Comments

'A delightful collection of stories involving Timothy Crumble and his family's adventures at Bodnant Garden. Nature, wildlife, fairies and trolls. Inspiriational to any child's imagination.'
Alison Owen. (Bakehouse Publications)

'A great read, which captures children's imagination.' *Sarah Rowlands. Parent, Conwy.*

'These stories really encourage children to look and listen and discover the locations in Bodnant Garden.' *Karen Follows. Deputy Head teacher, E. Sussex.*

'Timothy's adventures bring Bodnant's most magical places to life – just as I remember them when I was a child.'
Dr Heather Dyer. Royal Literary Fund Consultant Fellow. Children's author.

'I am so intrigued by these magical stories and am happy to have shared them with my younger sisters, Cadi, Elsi and Erin.'
Celyn Thomas-Jones, aged 11. Conwy.

TIMOTHY CRUMBLE EXPLORES BODNANT GARDEN
Anne Forrest

Dedication

For my grandsons, William and George
'You can be who you want to be. Believe in
yourselves.'

Disclaimer by the author, Anne Forrest.

These stories and any events taking place at the property of Bodnant Garden, Conwy Valley, North Wales, are fictitious and any factual content is from my own personal knowledge or understanding and they are published without input or endorsement from the National Trust.

Introduction

I hope you all enjoy the short stories and illustrations of *Timothy Crumble and the Explorers at Bodnant Garden.*

These stories are set in North Wales' Bodnant Garden. They were commissioned by Bodnant some time ago and were read to children at story-telling-time. The children could then look forward to trying to spot a troll, a fairy, the Laburnum Arch (which disappears in the winter!), the ha-ha, and the tallest tree in the whole of Britain. The stories had to be: 'informative, factual, educational and entertaining'.

Featuring Timothy Crumble and his family, they are suitable for anyone wanting to discover the garden through the eyes of a child – up to the age of 99 years old.

A garden can be large or small, and so can families; Timothy Crumble's family is just one type of many.

Look carefully at the illustrations and you will see something new each time, just as you will when exploring the 'flora and fauna' (the flowers, plants, and animals) in any garden.

Everyone is an individual, which means you are unique and have your own special ideas and opinions. When you explore Bodnant Garden, I hope you draw on these special skills to use your imagination. You may like to write your own stories, and draw your own pictures, so I have left some blank pages for you to do just that.

The six stories can be seen as stepping-stones. The first one is an introduction to Timothy Crumble, and to the Garden, with each subsequent story progressing to be of interest to older children, where I introduce some magical creatures and their habitats.

Timothy and Benji Crumble, their cousins, William, George, Anna and Ishbel Harker are fictitious, and so are their adventures, but they take place in a real setting in North Wales – and as much as these children would like to explore on their own, they must take an adult with them!

Glossary

READING TO A CHILD? I HOPE THIS WILL HELP YOUNGER CHLDREN WITH VOCABULARY.

Ajar	open slightly
Ancient	very old
Anthropomorphic	showing animal and human features
Audio	to be heard
Bark	surface of tree trunk
Century	a hundred years
Coffin	burial box
Compass	small instrument showing directions
Deceptive	different (from what you might see)
Determined	make a firm decision
Distraught	worried/sad
Dwarf	in this story, a small male creature
Emerge	appear into sight
Fictitious	not real, not true
Flora and fauna	plants and animals
Foraging	hunting/looking for
Gaze	to look
Habitat	a home, a house – a place to live
Ha-ha	a sunken trench
Hibernation	spending winter months in sleep
Hob-goblin	mischievous creature
Hue	colour (of)
Illustrate	picture
Incline	to raise
Interior	inside
Laburnum	tree with hanging, yellow flowers
Locate	exact position

Loftily	snooty (snootily)
Lysichiton Americanus	bad-smelling plant
Manoeuvre	a series of moves
Mausoleum	a burial chamber
Melancholy	sad/thoughtful
Morbid	an interest in unpleasant things
Mythical	(in children's stories) imaginary
Nooks & Crannies	small, hidden places
Paraphernalia	a collection of things
Project	a plan
RSPB	Royal Society – Protection of Birds
St David's Day (March 1st)	Wales' Patron Saint day
Daffodil	Wales' National Flower
Stalkers.	followers
Stench	really bad smell
Subsequent	happening after something, in time
Triumphantly	showing pleasure in winning
Trench	a ditch/a strip of dug-out of land
Troll	a mythical creature
Troupes	a group
Ultrasonic	a sound above human hearing
Unique	only one of its kind
Vivid Experience	strong image
Witnessed	seen by someone

List of Characters:

Timothy Crumble and
Benji, Timothy's baby brother.
Mr Tom and **Mrs Kate Crumble**, *their parents*

Timothy and Benji's cousins
William, George, Anna and **Ishbel**
Their parents: **Mr Brad** and **Mrs Prim Harker**, *who are*
Timothy and Benji's Uncle & Aunt

Here is a picture of Timothy (2nd on left), his mum, his baby brother, and his cousins.

Illustrated by Laura Stenhouse

Table of Contents

Comments...i

Dedication iv

Disclaimer by the author, Anne Forrest. v

Introduction.. vii

Glossary ix

List of Characters:.. xi

Map... xiv

TIMOTHY CRUMBLE AND HIS BROTHER BENJI 2

TIMOTHY CRUMBLE LOOKS FOR TROLLS 19

TIMOTHY CRUMBLE AND THE LOST ARCH.............31

TIMOTHY CRUMBLE GETS LOST!.............................43

TIMOTHY CRUMBLE HAS A NIGHT-TIME ADVENTURE
....63

TIMOTHY CRUMBLE AND THE EXPLORERS.............91

Author Biography 98

Illustrator Biography....................................99

Thanks 100

Map

Don't forget to pick up a helpful leaflet and map of the Garden from Reception, so you can spot the places mentioned in this book.

Timothy Crumble Explores Bodnant Garden

TIMOTHY CRUMBLE AND HIS BROTHER BENJI

Timothy Crumble had been visiting Bodnant Garden since he was a baby. 'In fact,' Timothy's mum said, 'You've been coming to Bodnant Garden since **before** you were born – we used to come when you were still in my tummy!'

'I don't remember that!' Timothy said. 'Not at all.'

'And now,' said Timothy's dad, 'We're taking your new baby brother to visit Bodnant. Aren't we, Benji?' He said this looking into the baby's carrycot, but Benji was fast asleep and did not hear their father.

Timothy was a bit fed up with this new baby in the Crumble family. He had been quite happy when it was just Mum, Dad and Timothy.

'Let's get going, then. We'll be there in less than half an hour,' said his mother. 'Timothy, do you remember us telling you about your first visit to the Garden? You lay in your pram under your red and white cover with your head on your red and white pillow. You could not take your gaze away from the tall trees above you as we pushed you along the pathway. Your wide-open eyes followed the shimmering sunlight as it sparkled

3

through the leafy branches. You loved to watch the light dancing its way down to say Hello, to you. Do you remember that Timothy?'

'No, I do not,' answered Timothy. 'Not at all!'

'Oh, but you must! You chuckled and gurgled at the light and tried to catch the sunbeams,' laughed his mother. 'And when you could talk, you said the twinkling lights looked like stars playing in the treetops.'

Timothy scowled. He didn't want to share his memories with his new baby brother, Benji. They were **his** memories.

They climbed into the car. What a lot of stuff they packed for this new baby. Timothy only needed his rucksack filled with a bottle of water, a few biscuits, a notepad for jotting things down, and coloured pencils in case he wanted to draw a picture.

'We've definitely got to take **all** Benji's paraphernalia,' explained his mum. 'He'll need his nappy changing and he'll want his feed.'

'Aren't we going to the café?' asked Timothy, looking shocked. 'We always have a cake at the café!'

'Of course we'll go to the café,' his mum answered. We'll still have our treat once we've finished our walk, but Benji can't eat cake – he'll want his bottle.'

'Phew!' said Timothy Crumble under his breath. He couldn't imagine not having a cake after their garden visit.

The car left the driveway, and as they set off, Timothy's mum and then his dad, kept reminding him of his favourite places in Bodnant Garden.

'Hey, what about the time when we three tried to hold hands and wrap ourselves around the huge oak tree just in front of the ha-ha, and mum became dizzy just looking up. And when mum asked if you'd like to sit on the topmost branches and look all around you like a king in his castle, you said, "Yes, yes, please, and can I wear a cloak and a crown!" You made us laugh a lot that day, Timothy.'

'Hmph!' was all Timothy said in reply.
'You must remember the ha-ha?'

'Ha-ha? No, I don't. Not at all.'

'Don't you remember dad falling into the ha-ha when he got too near? You had such a surprise when he disappeared before your eyes. Surely you remember that happening, Timothy? Especially when he popped up again.'

'You **must** remember the gardener coming up to dad and telling him that he **should not** go near the ha-ha, because it was out of bounds?'

'I'm afraid I don't,' said Timothy, loftily.

'Oh, dear,' said his mum. 'Your brain isn't working very well today, is it?'

'No, it is not. Not at all.'

But in his mind, Timothy couldn't help remembering the day they'd formed a chain as they held hands and tried to wrap themselves around the wide trunk of the big oak tree, and of the bright sunshine twinkling above him as he laughed into the high branches.

He **did** remember the ha-ha. Of course he remembered it. His dad had told him that a ha-ha was a deep ditch (or trench), dug out of the ground to separate the big lawn from the park so that sheep and cattle could stay where they were supposed to stay, instead of straying where they shouldn't be straying.

His dad had explained that a fence would have spoiled the lovely view, so the ditch (which is invisible from a distance) would do the trick.

They'd all agreed that 'ha-ha' was a strange name for a ditch which is used to keep animals from crossing from one field to another.

The Crumble family travelled in silence for a while and then Timothy's dad tried again. 'And what about all the other trees in Bodnant Garden, there are some very rare ones including the Giant Redwood. You remember us telling you that the Garden's Giant Redwood is the tallest tree in the whole of Britain, don't you, and that there are a few of them down in the Dell? They were planted about a hundred and sixty years ago, Timothy. Can you imagine as far back as one hundred and sixty years?'

'No, I can't imagine that at all,' he replied. 'Nor can I remember even a little bit about that tale!'

'Oh, dear,' said his mum, and trying again, she said, 'And what about your most favourite place of all – the Laburnum Arch! How you loved that cool, shady tunnel hanging with streamers of beautiful yellow flowers. Do you remember saying that the flowers looked like yellow rain as they hung above you, Tim?'

Timothy didn't answer but he did remember standing under the long tassels of yellow rain, which, in the breeze, swung and swayed until the flowers looked as if they dripped golden honey. He remembered that the long tassels cast a dappled light all over him.

'Surely you remember a little bit about the arch, Timothy?'

'No, I don't think I do!'

Mr and Mrs Crumble hoped Timothy would cheer up once they arrived at Bodnant. They hoped he would run as he usually did, through the tunnel, which had been built under the busy road. **Under** the road (so that visitors could enter the Garden safely).

Sure enough, as soon as they passed the Pavilion Tea Room, he raced ahead to come out into the familiar space next to the shop. On the way, he saw one of the gardeners, Graeme, working on the flower bed against the wall. Graeme pulled up bright green weeds and piled them high into his wheelbarrow.

'Hello, Timothy Crumble!' he called out. 'Nice to see you again. Hey, what this? A new baby? Is it a boy or a girl?'

Timothy didn't seem to hear the gardener ask about his new baby brother, he just called over his shoulder. 'Hi there, Graeme.'

'Wait for us,' called his dad.

'Yes,' pleaded his mum. 'Wait for Benji, Tim.'

At reception, Mrs Crumble showed their Family Ticket which allowed them to visit the garden as many times as they wished. Timothy and Benji's granddad had bought them one for Christmas again. 'Good old granddad,' their mum said. 'Aren't we lucky, boys?' And then she said, 'Would you like to push Benji in his pram, Tim?'

A little to his parents' surprise, Timothy suddenly **did** want to push Benji, he wanted to show him all he knew about Bodnant. So, having cheered up a bit, he put his hands around the pram's handle, and pushed it through the entrance for all prams and wheelchairs, and onwards towards the famous Laburnum Arch. He edged the pram so that Benji was right under the golden flowers which hung like yellow rain. Timothy saw Benji's face light up as if a sunbeam had kissed it.

'You've gone a sunshiny yellow!' he said to his brother and he laughed as the baby tried to reach out and touch the shimmering sunlight. Sharing is fun! thought Timothy.

'Look! Benji's trying to catch the sunbeams!' announced Timothy proudly. 'Isn't he a clever boy!' He then showed his baby brother the way the branches formed a brilliant arch of flowers above their heads, and how they looked as if they dripped golden honey.

They moved on, and when they got to the massive oak tree with the ha-ha to the left, and the grand Bodnant Hall across the lawn to the right, Timothy wanted to hold hands again and try to stretch their arms right around the tree's wide, wide girth.

'Let's get Benji out of his pram and hold his hands, too.'

'Yes, let's,' said his dad. So Benji was lifted out of the pram and together, they tried to reach around the tree, balancing Benji and holding his small arms out as wide as they'd go.

'No,' said Timothy. 'It's no good, we'll never do it. We'll have to wait until he and I are bigger – never mind, Benji, it was a good try.'

Benji was placed safely back in his pram, and Timothy whispered to him, 'When you **do** get bigger Benji, do you think you'd like to sit on the topmost branches and look all around as if you were a king in his castle, and wear a cloak and a crown?'

He then asked, 'Dad, will you fall into the ha-ha while Benji isn't looking, and pop up again? Please, please!'

'I'm afraid not Tim,' his dad said. 'I shouldn't have gone too near it last time. Ha-has are **not** for falling into. Not unless I want to get told off again by one of the gardeners!'

But Timothy and his mum turned the pram to face the field with the ha-ha sliced through it and told Benji all about the time Dad went too near, fell in, then looked as if he was buried up to his neck as he re-appeared. They all laughed aloud, Timothy louder than anyone else.

Eventually, they moved on and Timothy asked, 'Can we take Benji down into the Dell to see the Giant Redwood trees?'

'As long as we remember to use the suitable paths and avoid the steps!'

'Yes, I know that Dad.'

'Come along then, I may have to help you if we meet another pram or wheelchair.'

'O.K.' Timothy had really cheered up by now. 'I want to tell Benji that one of the redwoods is the tallest tree in Britain, and that they were planted here over one hundred and sixty years ago!' And so, he did.

Then, 'D'you think he'll remember all this information, Mum? D'you think he'll be able to imagine as far back as one hundred and sixty years?'

'I'm sure he will now you've told him, Timothy. I'm sure he'll remember all the information you've given him this afternoon, and because of that, who knows how his imagination will grow!'

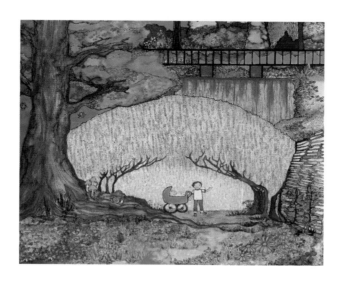

YOUR ACTIVITY PAGE

TIMOTHY CRUMBLE LOOKS FOR TROLLS

Timothy Crumble was a bit fed up. He had planned a day out at Bodnant Garden with his cousins, William and George – they were determined to find a troll! They'd read that trolls could be described as giants or dwarves, could be rather unpleasant-looking with broken stubby teeth, face warts, leathery ears, and crumpled-looking hats and tunics of green and brown and sometimes wore ill-matched socks! Often, they have crossed-eyes, long, dirty fingernails and choose to live in hillside caves or under bridges by the river. Ever since they'd read this, the boys were determined to find one in Bodnant Garden, because Timothy had seen just the home for a dwarf, hidden under a small stone bridge in the Dell.

The troll-stalkers had the whole day planned and ideally, would have liked to have this adventure on their own with no grown-ups in tow. But of course, they were not allowed to do that!

While Timothy's mum took his young brother Benji to his nursery school, William and George's mum and dad, Aunt Prim and Uncle Brad, volunteered to be in charge. That wasn't too bad, 'cause his aunt and uncle were good fun, but they also had to bring along Timothy's twin cousins, Anna and Ishbel. They were seven years old – and said they wanted to find a troll, too.

Yes, the boys were a bit fed up.

Anna and Ishbel had screeched and squealed all the way to Bodnant Garden because they didn't like the sound of a small hob-goblin-like creature that had long dirty fingernails, face-warts, broken stubby teeth, and ill-matched socks.

'So why do you want to look for one?' asked Timothy.

'Because we do!' answered Anna.

'Because we can, just as well as you can!' said Ishbel.

'Well, we don't want you to come with us.' The three boys all agreed with this.

'If the boys want to look for a troll, let them.' Aunt Prim joined in. 'Though I can't imagine what they're going to do with it, even if they do find one...'

As they all got out of the 4x4 car, Uncle Brad said, 'I think I might like to see a troll, too, d'you think I could join you boys?'

'Um...well...'

'No! No thank you, Uncle Brad. We'll be fine on our own,' said Timothy.

'Ah,' said Uncle Brad. 'I see. Fair enough. Perhaps you'll call out to me if you see one?'

'Sure!' answered the boys and raced ahead.

'I'll keep my eye on them, Prim,' whispered Uncle Brad. 'I'll not be **too** far behind in case they get too noisy in their excitement!' So, he followed at a safe distance and as he went, he said to Anna and Ishbel, 'You two call out to me as well if you see any...' and Aunt Prim led the girls towards the Upper Rose Terrace.

Anna and Ishbel had only walked a few yards along the stone terrace in front of Bodnant Hall, when Ishbel stopped in front of a handsome strawberry-coloured tree. This ancient plant was set here over a hundred years ago and leaned like an old lady against the walls; her red-barked arms stretched out as if to steady her, and at the base of her wide stem, a very fine set of rooms had been created. Two large areas looked as if they'd been carved out to house a family of small creatures.

'I 'spect a fairy lives in there,' Ishbel said.

'There looks to be room for more than one,' her mum agreed. 'What a grand home to have!'

Anna could see that something had been living inside. 'Look,' she pointed to the base of the rose tree. 'Acorns and nuts!'

'And bedding,' said her mum. 'Leaves and dried moss and sheep wool.' Soon, all three had seen signs of fairy life in the cave-like hole at the base of the rose stem and their mum told them that the rose had been planted here at Bodnant Garden, over a century ago!

On the way down to the Dell, they saw homes and houses that were very suitable for fairies: in the crumbling old walls, at the base of trees, and among the ferns and mosses. Red, yellow, white, and black toadstools looked ideal for use as chairs, tables, and beds.

Eventually they reached the bottom of the Dell and their mum said, 'I'm going to sit on this bench for a few minutes, you two can look around but **do not** go on the grass if there's a path to use. **Do not** go far, **do not** go near the river, and **do** be careful.' She sat and enjoyed the sound of the river bubbling and lapping the stones, a blackbird's sweet song, and a noisy woodpecker. The girls wandered a short distance and as they turned to come back to their mum, here, at the base of a reddy-brown Giant Redwood

23

tree, and almost hidden among the great roots, they saw a grand hallway that looked as if it'd been hollowed out of the soft bark. A kind of driveway led up through the old snowdrop-bed and opened into a small yard. The hinged hall door made of the same reddy-brown bark was slightly ajar, and as the girls tried to peer into it from the pathway, it snapped closed, shutting out the rest of the interior.

Just then, out of the woodland behind the tree, emerged a very strange looking creature. He was bent a little with age, was rather crooked, and wore a pointed hat which was scrunched down about his

24

leathery ears; his wrinkled face was dotted with warts and his teeth were broken and stubby; he wore a pair of silver-framed spectacles. The little troll didn't seem to notice Anna and Ishbel at all and hobbled up the tree's driveway.

Anna and Ishbel were so astonished, that they couldn't speak!

Bang, bang! The troll knocked on the door with the bone handle-head of his stick and it creaked open a crack to show the face of an elderly fairy.

'Good afternoon,' said the troll to her. 'I'm sorry to bother you without notice, but I've been driven from my home for the time being by three young human things – a boy child called Timothy and two others called William and George! Why, they've been poking a stick under the stone bridge and calling out as if they owned the place. I shan't put up with that!'

The fairy eased the bark door open a bit more to let him through.

'I shan't venture back there until those three have gone home - in fact, I've brought my overnight case!'

'You seemed to have packed in quite a hurry' said the fairy in her small, shaky voice. 'You've got half your stuff hanging out and look, you've dropped a yellow sock!'

'Never mind that, I've got a red one with me!' And the bent and crooked troll disappeared in through the tree's door. The old fairy stepped out, she looked right and left and right again, and then she pulled a shawl around her thin, fragile-looking wings, turned, and hobbled in after him.

Anna and Ishbel stood in amazement and before they could take all this in, the door seemed to melt into the base of the Giant Redwood, and it was difficult for them to see where it had been. Just to the left of the tree's roots, Ishbel saw a small flash of lemon on the ground. She reached over from the pathway and there was the tiniest sock of the brightest yellow! She put it in her pocket.

When Anna and Ishbel returned to their mum, they didn't tell her anything of the fairy or the troll, they were too surprised to have witnessed such a thing.

When they met the boys up by the turnstile exit, they were still a bit unsure of what they'd seen, so said nothing once more.

The boys had plenty to say!

'We didn't clap eyes on a troll! Not one!'

'Not even when we poked about under the stone bridge with a stick where we **know** one of them lives!'

'We'll have to try again!'

'How did you two, get on?' asked the girls' father putting an arm around each of their shoulders as they stood side by side. 'See anything interesting?'

Ishbel looked at Anna and Anna looked at Ishbel, she placed her hand into her sister's pocket and fingered the tiny yellow sock.

YOUR ACTIVITY PAGE

TIMOTHY CRUMBLE AND THE LOST ARCH

Timothy Crumble and his cousins, William and George Harker, had their birthdays within days of each other.

'What a coincidence!' said their mothers: 'And how very convenient. We can have one birthday treat to cover all three boys!'

'Hmmm…' said the boys, not sure if this was a good idea at all.

This year, it was decided that a morning trip to the Cinema, a picnic lunch at the nearby RSPB Nature Reserve where the boys loved birdwatching, and Bodnant Garden in the afternoon would suit everyone. And to add to the adventure, they would travel by bus!

The bus stopped right outside the grounds of Bodnant Garden where Mrs Crumble, Mrs Harker and the three boys got off. All the way from the coast, Timothy had not stopped talking about his favourite places in Bodnant. William and George had their favourites too: William wanted to see some of the tallest trees in Great Britain – the Giant Redwood. He also wanted them to reach around the huge oak tree near the ha-ha by stretching their clasped hands around the wide, wide girth. They'd never managed it yet!

George was keen to find the little stone bridge to see if he could spy the troll which he **knew** lived there somewhere underneath or thereabouts.

Timothy wanted to show his cousins the *Cats of Bodnant* graves lying under the huge, dark limbs of the Old English Yew tree, and his most favourite place of all - the famous Laburnum Arch where their faces would become a golden sunshiny colour when, in the bright mid-afternoon, their upturned faces would take on the hue of the yellowy flower tassels dripping like warm honey.

'The Arch is first on the list,' cried Timothy as he raced through the underground tunnel with William and George hot on his heels.

'Then the Redwoods,' said William, running after him.

'Then the trolls!' said his brother George, catching up with them.

While the mums showed their Family Membership cards at the desk, the boys checked their rucksacks: bottled water, notebook, pencils, coloured pens, and maps. In addition, each boy had received a compass for their birthday because they had just joined an orienteering group and were keen on exploring.

'We'll never get lost if we have a compass,' said William, who was older than

Timothy by two days. 'We can use them to navigate our way around as long as we know where North is and...'

'We know all that...' said Timothy and George together, impatient to get going.

The three boys flew through the doors, and with Timothy in the lead, headed left up the pathway to the Laburnum Arch.

Mrs Crumble and Mrs Harker strolled a few minutes behind them and when they got to the entrance of the Arch, were astounded to see Timothy Crumble standing stock-still with his mouth open in surprise. In fact, Timothy could not speak for some minutes.

'Something wrong?' asked his mum.

'You ok, Tim?' asked his aunt.

William and George looked all around, puzzled.

Timothy was looking up anxiously at where he expected to see golden festoons of graceful flowers swaying in the breeze: festoons of honey-coloured blooms laden with buzzing bees searching for nectar, and curtains of yellow rain dripping with gold, casting sunny shadows and dappled light at his feet.

Instead, all he could see was a frame of dry, skinny, brown branches tied neatly with small bits of string. It looked as if a plain wicker-basket roof had been draped overhead and down the tunnel-shaped frame. Not a golden petal, not a green bud, not a peep of yellow rain.

Eventually, Timothy whispered hoarsely, 'Where's the Arch? What's happened to it? It's gone! It's been lost!'

'Gone?'

'Lost?'

'Whatever do you mean, Timothy?'

'Can't you see? Any of you?'

'What?'

'The Arch! It's gone! Disappeared! Lost!'

Just then, the gardener, Graeme, popped up from the wide flower bed by the wall. 'What's the problem, boys?'

'Can't you see?'

Graeme looked at Timothy, then at William and George, then at the two mums. 'Sorry,' he said... 'But what exactly is the trouble?'

Everyone stared at Timothy who seemed to be struck dumb. 'I, well... I... what have you done with the Laburnum Arch?' he said accusingly. 'Have you lost it?'

'Lost it?' Graeme frowned. 'Um... er... well, no, of course not.'

Graeme's glance went from the small group along the length of the tunnel.

'Why, it's here, where it always is. It's just having a bit of rest, storing up all its energy for later in the year. Look, come here and I'll show you the tiny buds just peeking.' And he pointed them out among the intricate wicker-woven patterns.

Timothy could not believe that these bony, twisted brown sticks would transform into the rich, golden curtain with which he was so familiar.

'But these are like witches' fingers! Witches' fingers and toes creeping all over each other and pointing in every direction with their long nails! No way will these turn into the Laburnum Arch!'

Graeme saw Timothy's distraught face. 'Hey, now,' he said. 'Trust me. You come back in a couple of months and see if I'm right, eh?'

'You mean, the Arch **isn't** lost?'

'No, not at all!'

'It's just hiding in these bare twigs?'

'That's correct. Just hiding!'

'Phew!' Timothy Crumble said with relief.

'It's a date, then,' the two mums said in unison. 'We'll be back in a few months' time.'

'Phew,' said William and George.

'Phew,' Timothy said again. 'That's ok, then. Come on, William, let's go and see the Giant Redwoods.'

'And then we can look for that troll!' said George running behind them, out into the airy garden...

YOUR ACTIVITY PAGE

Timothy Crumble Explores Bodnant Garden

TIMOTHY CRUMBLE GETS LOST!

Timothy Crumble will never forget the day he got lost at Bodnant Garden!

It was a bright, Spring day and he was with his mum and cousins, William and George. The boys whizzed through the Laburnum Arch which was just beginning to show off its blossom of yellow flowers that hang down like golden rain.

The snowy-white snowdrops were just about finished in the fields and on the lawn, where they drooped their brave little bell-like heads and returned their energy into the ground for next year's display. Now daffodils had taken over! Three or four different shades of yellow heads swayed and ran in drifts over the land at Bodnant, looking as if trumpets were being blown in the breeze. Mrs Crumble suggested that the boys tried to count how many species of daffodils had been planted over the years. They found creamy-white narcissus and pale lemony jonquils; under the trees and on the banks were the tiniest, most delicately rich yellow, flute-like flowers of the dwarf daffodil.

'Aren't they a sight,' said one of the visitors to Mrs Crumble. 'We never tire of seeing the daffs looking so cheerful. Despite the cold winter, the early flowering ones

43

were out in time for St David's Day on March 1st!'

Mrs Crumble stood gazing at this sight and let the boys run ahead. 'Be careful, you three,' she called over her shoulder. And as she always did, she said. 'Stay together now!'

She caught up with the boys down in the Dell, just as they'd crossed the little bridge where elegant waterside plants grew against the wall; these yellow stately-looking plants were called, *Lysichiton Americanus*. But looks were deceptive as the boys well knew and this was half the attraction!

'How extraordinary,' stated Mrs Crumble, 'That such a fine and noble-looking plant should smell so disgusting!' She watched the boys approach the plants cautiously and then heard them explode with sounds of disgust as the strong-smelling, decaying vegetation reached their noses.

'Ugh, no wonder they call them 'skunk cabbage', said George.

'It's **so** stinky!'

'Urrr-gh!'

'It's gro-oss!'

The boys had heard more than once the explanation of why this plant smelled so badly: the rotting stench attracts midges, beetles, and other insects and when the insects go from flower to flower, they take the pollen with them, thus the plant is fertilised and enabled to make seeds.

Knowledge of how new plants were created did not stop the boys from acting silly though.

'It smells like poo!' shrieked George loudly, and all three ran like the wind as far away as they could, shouting and laughing at the horror of it all. And then returned to the plants for **more** terrible smells!

'Quiet!' said Timothy's mum in a loud whisper. 'Visitors are trying to enjoy the peace here!' and she steered them back over the stone bridge (the one that looked as if a dwarf troll might live underneath it). 'And **do** stop that ridiculous giggling!' Timothy's mum sounded a bit cross.

Eventually they decided to return to the tea-room for cake.

When Mrs Crumble saw the boys going up the more difficult pathway, she said, 'I think I'll take the easy way back,' and choosing to walk up the gentler path, she said under her breath, 'I could do with a bit of peace and quiet,' then she called out, 'Keep together, boys. See you at the top.'

'OK, Mum,' Timothy said over his shoulder.

'Will do, Aunt Kate!' shouted William and George.

The lads raced up the path and Mrs Crumble enjoyed her peaceful stroll up the gentle slope. She stopped to listen to a blackbird singing and heard another return his song.

Lovely! And she settled on one of the benches for a rest. Suddenly, William and George appeared: they were breathless.

'Timothy ran ahead, and now we can't find him!' William announced.

'He ran ahead!' echoed George. 'We couldn't see him, so we decided to come and find you, Aunt Kate.'

'Well done,' said their aunt. 'Very well done, you two, let's hurry along so that we can all meet up again.'

But before they moved, they called out, three times, 'Timothy!' But no-one replied. They heard a raven call, and then there was silence again.

'He's bound to be up by the exit', said George. 'He has his compass with him.'

So, they made their way towards the place where they fully expected to see Timothy, safe and sound.

On the way, Mrs Crumble and her nephews stopped to talk to the large, ginger-coloured cat who was unsurprisingly called 'Ginger'; he was basking in a sunny spot just out of their reach, and then they saw another cat coming to join him. They had to look twice at Whisky before they realised he only had three legs – but despite that, he walked very well!

The three made their way past the grand Hall and towards the turnstile exit. Hmm, still no sign of Timothy, so they decided to go to the reception area and ask if any one of the staff had seen him there. All the staff and volunteers wear a badge so that they can be approached for help at any time.

'No,' said the girl at the desk, 'Timothy certainly hasn't come this way!'

One of the volunteers recognised George: 'Hello, George,' he said. 'You look a bit worried.'

'We've lost our cousin,' George told him.

'Oh, I don't think he's lost, George,' said his aunt Kate. 'Timothy knows the garden well...but, oh dear, where is he...?' and they all looked about as if they expected to see Timothy's head pop up from behind the desk. But there was no sign of him.

'Ah, let's get searching, then,' the receptionist said, and immediately used her walkie-talkie phone to alert the Bodnant guides that a small boy was lost in the Garden.

Soon, three of the guides appeared with their badges on and a walkie-talkie phone each. 'You stay here, George,' suggested their aunt Kate. 'He'll be glad to see you here if he comes this way. William and I will go with the guides.'

'That's fine,' agreed the receptionist.

'Yes,' said the guide to Mrs Crumble. 'What a good idea; you and William can stay on the top lawn where you'll see him if he comes up any of the pathways; one of us will go towards the Rose Terrace, the other towards the ha-ha and Oak tree, and I'll go down towards the Dell.'

And off they went, spreading out like a fan in three directions to try to locate Timothy Crumble.

William and his aunt stood watching all the different paths from which Timothy might appear. William's eyes grew sore as he looked and looked and looked. No Timothy! They both heard the guides calling, 'Timothy, Timothy, Timothy Crumble!' They saw the guides asking other visitors, 'Have you seen a young boy looking a bit lost?'

'Timothy! Timothy…!'

But he knows the garden well, thought Mrs Crumble to herself, although I don't think he's been up that path on his own before... Oh, dear, I shouldn't have allowed it… What can have happened to him?

They heard the guides calling from different parts of the garden: from the terrace, from the lily pond, from the round garden, but they did not hear anybody answer and they grew very worried indeed.

*

Timothy **certainly** had not used that path before on his own! After leaving his mum and speeding ahead of his cousins, he had raced up quite happily, taking the stone steps easily; he'd passed the large flat boulders on his right and sat on the seat for a short while, looking down, down, down into the Dell, seeing the visitors like small insects in the distance. He'd then followed the pretty little path upwards until he came to a stream with water scuttling over the stones and forming small deep pools. The clatter of water running and chuckling over the stones sounded to Timothy as if it were laughing! Joining in, he laughed too at this and started to cross the stream using the big stepping-stones in the middle of the dark pool.

From this view-point he could see upstream and downstream and couldn't help thinking about the time he'd come to Bodnant Garden with William and George's twin sisters, Anna and Ishbel. They were seven years old and had told Timothy and their brothers that they thought fairies lived in the Garden! The boys had not been too sure about this, but Timothy had to admit that this was **just** the place that might house fairies very comfortably indeed! In fact, it seemed perfect with small nooks and crannies in the rocks, deep recesses behind the young fern-tree growth, a small cave-like place just behind the small waterfall and even a village green of moss for them to meet and have parties among the toadstools!

It was still and quiet except for the fall of water, and Timothy decided to sit down and rest awhile. It was so peaceful by the stream that he found his eyes closing in sleep but snapped them open again just in time to see a small, winged creature stepping lightly over the moss, she was wearing ballerina slippers, a cap made of leaves, and she carried a shopping basket. She pulled aside a delicate water fern and quickly disappeared beyond the plant.

He blinked twice in surprise and saw the fern gently sway back into place like a curtain. A few minutes later she re-appeared, this time with an elderly fairy who had a shawl wrapped around her winged shoulders despite the mild afternoon; the young fairy pointed out the tiny violets nestling among the mosses. The old fairy peered closely at the violets and nodded. Timothy stayed incredibly still.

Wow, he thought, Am I seeing things? The sound of the chuckling water lulled him into closing his eyes again, and when he next opened them he did not know if he'd been asleep for two minutes or half an hour, but he knew he'd had a vivid experience.

He looked around. 'Oh, no! Where's Mum? Where're William and George?' When Timothy realised that he was not where he was supposed to be, he panicked, shot up and ran! Upwards he went following the stone steps and then came to a small T-junction where he could have gone left or right. Left would have taken him up towards the front lawn and Bodnant Hall, and from there, he would have seen the familiar area which would have led him towards the exit or reception. Instead (and I suppose it was an easy mistake to make after the shock of seeing two fairies by the stream), he took the path to the right and continued running, probably not concentrating at all! He was thinking about what he'd just seen and what he would – or **would not** – tell his cousins in case they thought he was making up such a story; and he worried about not meeting his mum as promptly as he'd promised.

He followed the path along, still running, and before he realised where he was going, the path had taken him downwards back towards the Dell. He turned and took the nearest path but that led to a roped-off area *Please Do Not Cross this Rope*. He raced back and soon, every path he saw looked like the previous one and he could not tell **where** he was. He heard someone shout: 'Timothy, Timothy, Timothy Crumble,' but as he answered with, 'Yes, here I am!' a raven squawked twice, very loudly, from somewhere nearby, drowning out his voice, and then there was silence. He started to cry, and his head became full of frightening thoughts – he knew he was being silly, but he couldn't stop thinking frightening thoughts.

Visitors passed him by, but because Timothy didn't want anyone to see that he was crying or to know he'd got himself lost, he ran as if he knew where he was heading.

Of course, poor Timothy had panicked! If he had been able to stop and calmly allow his thoughts to collect themselves, he would have remembered the compass in his rucksack! He would have known that to get to the exit, he should make his way **upwards** at every opportunity, not downwards. Upwards would have led to the exit or to the reception near the Laburnum Arch – and there he would have found his mum, his cousins and the guides looking out for him.

*

One of the guides had made her way down towards the Dell and there, standing alone, under a huge Giant Redwood tree, she saw a boy looking **very** small and very lost. She called, 'Timothy!' and saw him spin round and back again as if he did not know where the sound came from. 'Timothy?' she called again, this time a little louder, and saw a tearful, pink face turn towards her. 'Hello, young man! Are you Timothy Crumble?'

She saw him nod hesitantly, then she saw him recognise the Bodnant Garden badge she was wearing on her jacket, and then he made his way towards her.

'Hello,' she said into her walkie-talkie phone, 'I've found him. Tell his mum he's ok. We'll be up at reception in a short while.'

On their way up, the guide told Timothy that if ever he lost his way again in Bodnant

Garden, he should take an **upwards** path where he would find a familiar place or two. 'And,' she added, 'you must look out for a guide or a gardener wearing a Bodnant badge; there are a few of us around, always walking about to see if anyone needs help. Don't forget, Timothy, make your way upwards, and look out for a badge-wearing guide!'

Before he knew it, Timothy Crumble was being hugged by his mum and by William and George who had just wiped a very worried look from their faces!

George felt he had to ask, 'Why didn't you use your compass, Tim?'

Before Timothy could think of an answer, his mum said, 'Come on, Mr Explorer.' And to the three boys, Mrs Crumble confirmed, 'There are a few lessons to be learned from this afternoon. We'll discuss them after we've had a piece of cake at the Tea Room!'

All three boys raced off towards the underground tunnel and the Pavilion Tea Room, but Mrs Crumble noticed that Timothy didn't run too far ahead!

Timothy Crumble Explores Bodnant Garden

YOUR ACTIVITY PAGE

TIMOTHY CRUMBLE HAS A NIGHT-TIME ADVENTURE

Timothy Crumble will always remember the day at Bodnant Garden which led to a night-time adventure!

It was during the Autumn half-term break from school. The weather was fine, and he was with his mum and his cousins, William and George.

'We've got the whole day to ourselves,' the boys said, rummaging in their rucksacks. Map, compass, binoculars, notebook, pens and pencils tumbled about next to drink-bottles and snacks.

'Yes,' said Timothy's mum. 'The whole day, so let's make the most of it.'

Every time they came to Bodnant they noticed something different, something new. Last time, it was a stone statue that none of the Crumble family had ever seen before, it was hidden within a large rosy-pink camellia against a stone wall – quite camouflaged! Today, the boys decided that they would try to spot as many stone statues as they could and record them in their notebooks. In the end, William spotted one more than Timothy and George.

After they'd completed this project, the boys raced ahead to see the ha-ha and to hug the huge oak tree, to see if their arms could stretch all the way around the wide trunk. 'No way!' George said. 'Not even if we had Tommy and Henry from school with us. No way could we reach all around!' And off they ran again, with Timothy's mum calling, 'Wait for me!'

She caught up with them as they came upon the pets' graveyard. Under a huge gnarled Old English Yew tree, the mighty branches dipping low and dark, the boys stood silently. It was eerily quiet, the only sound was the stream gurgling into the pond and out again on its way to the little river called, *Hiraethlyn*.

They all looked at the two grand stone slabs lying at their feet.

Antonia of Bodnant 1948-1952. Cat to the McLarens

Mr Kipps of Bodnant 1943-1956. Cat to the McLarens.

'Cats of Bodnant!' murmured Mrs Crumble.

'What great looking gravestones,' said William. 'For cats! They must have been **very** splendid cats...'

'Very special,' agreed George.

'Oh, dear', said Timothy soberly, thinking about the dead cats.

'Oh, it was a long, long time ago', Mrs Crumble said. 'Bodnant has had many pets since then.'

'Did they bury people here, too, Mum?'

'Timothy! You're **so** morbid!'

'Well, I just thought that if they buried the cats here, they might also bury the family...'

Mrs Crumble suddenly remembered the mausoleum, mysteriously named, The Poem. 'Ah, well, you're not too far away from the truth there, Tim. A long time ago, they did bury people here, not actually in the ground, but they placed the coffins in a memorial building, called a mausoleum.'

'Oh!' said William. 'That's weird'.

'That's gruesome!' said George.

'But that's what some people did a long, long time ago.'

'Where about in the Garden is it?'

'Look at your maps.'

The boys poured over their maps and saw that they could reach it on a pathway towards The Waterfall.

'Here it is!'

'But it's called, 'The Poem', here!'

'Yes.'

'Why? It doesn't make sense!'

'Well, it would if you think about what the name **might** mean. No-one is sure but it's believed to stand for 'Place Of Eternal Memory'.

'Oh,' said William. 'That does make sense.'

'Oh!' said Timothy. 'That's quite nice.'

'Oh!' said George. 'I guess so! Can we go back and look at it?'

'Next time,' Mrs Crumble said. 'We'll do that next time. Come on; let's see who gets to the Round Garden first, and then it's lunch at the café.' And so, the buried cats and the coffins in the Poem forgotten, the boys bounded off and up the pathway in a much more cheerful mood.

They got to the Round Garden with the fountain (the one where the stone dolphins in the centre balanced the fluted plate on their tails) and Timothy announced that he wanted to count how many small box-shrubs had been planted around the fountain. He was in a competitive mood and William was quick to accept the challenge. 'Yes, lets.' He turned to a fresh page in his notebook and licked his pencil.

'Bor-ing!' said George. 'I want to look for a troll.'

'Later,' said Mrs Crumble who took the opportunity to sit down on the wooden bench and enjoy the sound of the water as it spewed and splashed over the scalloped edges into the pond.

Just beyond the fountain, Jo, the gardener, was tending some unruly shrubs, pruning, and tying them into a good shape. Eventually, the boys sat alongside Mrs Crumble to drink their bottled water and to check their calculations again. It was thirsty work counting statues and box hedges.

They looked dreamily into the shrubbery, admiring the colours: deep pink, green, bluey-green, and greeny-blue, and even turquoise. It reminded them of one of the most colourful creatures to live at Bodnant Garden: George the peacock who had loved to spread his tail, called a 'train', in a huge fan. Sadly, he and his pea-hen wife had since died. When Jo, the gardener, heard them talking about the peacock, she said quietly, 'Old George is still missed by a lot of people. It's such a pity he died, but these things *do* happen, you know'.

'Yes, we do know,' said William thinking of the pets' graves.

'Yes,' said Timothy thinking about The Poem.

'Where is George the peacock buried?' asked George.

'Ah, somewhere at Bodnant, but I don't think his grave is quite as splendid as the cats'!

They sat in silence for a minute; the boys looked thoughtful.

'Well, come now, how do you think we can best remember George?' said Mrs Crumble, trying to shake them out of a melancholy mood. 'He deserves to be remembered in a big way,'

'I think I'll draw a picture with his train fanned right out, and colour him in,' Timothy decided. 'I can remember all the different blues and greens and those lovely eyes all over his train.'

All the boys joined in:

'Oh, do you remember how he used to strut around with his fan waving and swaying and quivering?'

'And showing off!'

'He was very proud of his train, wasn't he?'

'Yes. I've never seen a peacock quite so proud as George was!'

'Is that why they say, 'as proud as a peacock?'

'It certainly is,' answered Mrs Crumble.

'I'm going to make a clay model of George, colour him, and fire him in our kiln at home,' announced William.

'I think you've chosen lovely ways to remember George the peacock,' Jo said from behind the shrubs.

Just then, a very large ginger cat appeared, she seemed to be stalking the land with her tail in the air, she looked at nothing in particular as if she wasn't interested in anybody or anything, but Timothy noticed that she kept a keen eye on them as she sidled around the wooden legs of the bench.

'Oh, you've found Ginger!' Jo said. 'Always on the hunt for a tasty morsel is Ginger; the mice keep their distance when **she's** around!'

'You're beautiful,' Mrs Crumble said to Ginger, trying to stroke her.

Suddenly as if from nowhere, another cat appeared – his name was Whisky, and strangely enough, only had three legs but could get around just as well as Ginger.

'Oh, you've arrived too, have you,' Jo said, smiling at the sight of Whisky. And to the boys, she said. 'Do you remember the cat called Bonkers?'

They laughed, remembering how Mrs Crumble had thought they were describing the cat in an unkind way. 'She doesn't look bonkers,' she had said.

'Well, she **is** Bonkers', the gardener had said.

'She doesn't look at all bonkers to me!' Mrs Crumble had told the boys. 'Nor strange in any way at all. In fact, she looks to be a **very** fine cat indeed'.

'No, no, no!' the gardener had explained, quickly. She's not **actually** bonkers. Bonkers is her **name**!'

This made them all laugh, as they made their way to the Pavilion Tea-room.

*

Timothy's dad joined them for the afternoon at Bodnant Garden, and he had a plan.

'It's a good thing you've packed your binoculars,' he told the boys.

'Why?' George asked.

'You'll soon see. 'Come on, we've got an appointment.'

'Who with?' William asked.

'Guess.' said his uncle.

The boys spent the next five rowdy minutes trying to guess with whom they had an appointment, and by the time they'd reached reception, they'd given up, and looked exasperated.

Timothy's dad said, 'Ah, here's our appointment! He's a friend of mine and one of the guides who knows a lot about birds. He's taking us bird-spotting.'

'Hi there,' said the guide. 'I'm Denny.' He pointed to his Bodnant Garden guide badge. 'I'm not on duty just now, but I hear you'd like to spot birds with me.

'Great,' said Timothy, checking to see if he had his binoculars handy. 'Let's do it!'

'OK.' Denny said. 'Welcome to Bodnant Garden. Now, the first thing you need is the *Birds of Bodnant* check-list. Did you know that 60 different species of birds have been spotted here following a two years' survey?'

'Wow', Timothy whispered to his dad. 'It looks as if we've got our work cut out today!'

'Ah, I don't think we'll be expected to spot 60 different birds in one go, Tim. The birds were seen at different times of the year. We'll just do our best, eh?'

Soon, Timothy had ticked off a blackbird, a robin, two magpies, a house sparrow, a blue tit, and a great tit. They were easy to spot because they felt so at home at Bodnant, they didn't take any notice of humans at all, they just flitted and swooped and landed wherever they fancied.

Suddenly, the guide lifted his hand, 'Can you hear that?' They all stopped to listen carefully.

'I can't hear a thing,' Timothy said, 'Except people's voices and a machine, somewhere in the distance.'

'Ah, but are you *really* listening?' the guide said. 'Often people listen but don't really hear.'

'How do they do that?' asked George.

'How **can** they do that?' asked William. 'I mean, listen and not hear?'

'I'll try and show you.' Denny put up the palm of his hand, as if to say, 'stop', and a finger to his lips as if to say, 'be quiet for a minute'.

The boys concentrated hard and as the silence grew around them, a definite sound came from one of the large shrubs; they all peered at the branches. The silence became louder (yes, a silence can be loud – just you try it sometime), and in amongst that silence, a high-pitched 'tsee, tsee, tsee,'

came from the tree, and then another high-pitched 'tee-lee-de, tee-lee-de, tee-lee-de.'

Timothy's dad asked the guide, quietly, 'How did you hear those small sounds above all the other noises?'

'Ah,' Denny answered. 'My ears are tuned to *every* bird call. And I can identify each one.'

'Each one?'

'Yes, each one. I can tell if it's a call, a song, or a warning cry. I can tell if it's a male, female or juvenile.'

'Wow,' said Timothy Crumble.

'I can also tell if it's a winter song or a summer song.'

'How?' asked Timothy.

'By learning to hear – listening properly to each bird's voice.'

'Wow!' Timothy said again. 'That's amazing. Will I be able to do that, too?'

'Of course you will, you can do anything you want to if you really try.'

'Anything?'

'Anything!' The guide saw Timothy looking a bit doubtful. 'I promise you,' he said again. 'If you want to know about birds, you can do so.'

'We do know a bit, 'cause we go to the RSPB Nature Reserve and watch birds from the hides.'

'Well, you're halfway there already, Timothy. You go to the RSPB, you have a fine pair of binoculars, a bird check-list, and I'll bet you have a bird book at home, somewhere.'

'Yes, we have. I had one from my granddad for Christmas.'

'Well, done,' said the guide. 'Now, we'd better see what bird is singing so very loudly in that bush.' And he trained his eyes upwards, listening again. 'Tee-lee-de, tee-lee-de, tee-le-dee.'

'I can't see a thing,' said William.

'Nor me,' said George.

'I must admit,' said Mrs Crumble. 'Neither can I.'

'Not a thing!' said Timothy Crumble as he swept his binoculars along the branches.

'Ah, but are you looking?' asked Denny.

'Yes, of course.'

'Really looking? Often, people look but don't really see. It's a bit like listening and hearing, it's sometimes not done properly! Right, now concentrate on that branch to the left, the one just above the fork in the shrub halfway up...' They did so, peering through their binoculars.

'Keep looking... fix your eyes on where you can hear the song.' The sound of the bird-song got louder and more than one of the same bird joined in. It seemed ages before a movement was spotted among the leaves. 'Can you see...?'

'There it is,' said Timothy's mum in a low voice. 'There.' She pointed, and everyone looked earnestly into the shrub with great concentration, and as if by magic, four small birds came into view – they'd been there all the time.

'Wow, they're so tiny. What are they?'

'They're Goldcrests; the smallest bird in Britain!'

'I thought the wren was the smallest!' Timothy said, 'I thought the Jenny Wren was the smallest bird in Britain!'

'Ah,' said the guide. 'Now you know it's the Goldcrest.'

'But its song is so loud for such a tiny bird!'

'Hmmmm,' said Timothy's dad. 'That's very often the case. Small things **can** make a lot of noise!'

Half an hour later, Timothy's check-list was growing as he'd ticked off fifteen different species of birds, including a pair of buzzards high in the sky, swallows with long tail streamers swooping and swerving through the air and wagtails bobbing and running all over the lawn – and even a dipper feeding her fat baby beneath the waterfall on the water's edge.

Suddenly, the guide leapt up from where they were taking a rest and put his binoculars up to his eyes. 'Well, I'll be blowed,' he said. 'Just look at that. A Red Kite! Two of them! What a thing to see here in the Conwy Valley!'

Timothy said, 'They fly like a real kite!'

'Yes,' his dad said. 'Just one flick of its tail and it rears off just like your blue and green kite does when we're in the field!'

Denny was very excited and explained that red kites almost became extinct until in 1989, when young kites from Europe were introduced into Britain, and now there are over 1,000 pairs in the country, with more than 500 of them in Wales.

'They've been seen in the Conwy Valley for the last couple of years,' he said. 'But it's still a rare sight here.'

'So, rare,' Timothy said, triumphantly (he was very pleased with himself). 'They're not even on the check-list!'

'Well spotted,' said the guide. 'You can all add the red kite to your list now. And I think I can safely say that you've beaten the check-list by one species of bird. Yes, very well done, Timothy, William and George!'

*

Timothy's dad had another plan. But he wasn't going to tell them until tomorrow.

*

It was about 4.30 the next afternoon when Timothy's dad said, 'We four are going out. Get your coats and hats and make sure Benji's wrapped up well.

Mrs Crumble looked very puzzled. 'But the sun's almost setting. It'll soon be dark! Where on earth are we going?'

'It's a surprise,' he said. And wouldn't say another word about it.

The Crumble family's car soon took them on a familiar road, and they parked just inside the car park at Bodnant Garden.

Timothy saw Bodnant staff and some volunteer guides leaving the garden after their day's work. Very puzzled, he said. 'But it's closed! Why are we here?'

'Wait and see,' his dad replied.

Just then another car's headlight swept into the car park, turned around, and came to a stop alongside. Uncle Brad and Aunt Prim waved at Timothy, and then his cousins waved excitedly, too.

'It's William and George,' shouted Timothy. 'And Anna and Ishbel! What are we all doing here?'

Suddenly, everybody was out of their cars and such a noise broke out. Can you imagine how loud they sounded as they all questioned Timothy's dad?

He put up the palm of his hand and a finger to his lips, just as Denny had done when he wanted them to stop, and to be quiet.

'Now,' he said, in a whisper. 'We're going to listen and look for signs of life in the garden.

'But we can't see anything!'
'It's getting too dark!'

'And Bodnant is closed! How are we going to get in?'

'We're not **going in**.'

'That's silly, Dad! how can we see anything in the garden if we can't get in?'

'We're going to try out the skills my friend Denny told us about.'

'What d'you mean?'

'You remember he told us that if we **really** listened, we might hear more, and if we **really** look, we may see more?'

'Yes,' said Timothy.

'Yes,' said William. 'I remember that.'

'Ye-es,' said George, hesitantly. 'So do I but how are we going to do this in the dark?'

'Let's wait and see, shall we? First I just want to tell you all to stay close to each other, and to do as you're told. I'll lead the way and Uncle Brad will stay at the back to make sure everyone keeps together.'

All around them, the light started to fade, and everyone was surprised when their eyes became accustomed to it.

George announced, 'It's already working! I can see better than I could when we first arrived.'

'And look at Benji's eyes,' William said. 'They're wide open and the whites are very white as he's trying to see.'

And sure enough, Benji gazed up into the darkness and the whites of his eyes seemed to shine in the dark.

Ishbel wondered out aloud to Anna if there might be ghosts at Bodnant, but

Timothy said there were no such things as ghosts!

He'd just finished saying that, when a white shape swooped out of the nearby trees with a crazy kind of shriek and flew above their heads, up and over the wall into the garden.

'It's a ghost!' cried Timothy amid the squeals and shouts of 'No way!' from his cousins.

Once they'd all calmed down, his Uncle Brad said. 'It's OK, Tim, it's only an owl. A Barn Owl.'

'How d'you know?'

'Well, I could see his white chest-feathers and those on the underside of his wings very clearly in the dark, **and** I could hear his call; I don't think he hoots like other owls do.'

'So, you can see and hear better in the dark, Uncle Brad?'

'Not better, but I noticed something I wouldn't have done so easily in the daylight – his white feathers. And I heard the call he made. Different owls make different calls.'

He went on. 'Y'know, I'm very surprised to see a Barn Owl here, the owls who live at Bodnant are mostly Tawny Owls.'

Every now and again, Timothy's dad put up his hand, and cupped his other hand behind his ear. That made them all stop and incline their heads to concentrate on listening. They were surprised at how many different noises the owls make! A whistle-kind of call, a yelp, a bark, and a sharp, beak-snap.

'We'd have to do a lot of studying to identify which owl is which.' Timothy said.

'Yes. I guess so,' his dad replied. 'But just think about it. Tonight, you've identified a Barn Owl because of its white feathers, and you've heard a few others which, because they are usually night-birds, you probably wouldn't see or hear them during the day. I remember an old saying, something like: "An owl heard, is an owl seen", that's because it's very good at camouflaging itself, so not easily spotted.'

They walked all around the car park and along the footpaths; they watched a family of rabbits playing on the slopes and Ishbel said she saw the rabbits' eyes shining in the headlights of passing cars.

Later, nearer the woods, George said he saw a fox standing as still as a statue, and saw his eyes blink, before stealthily creeping into the hedgerow, its tail low.

William thought he heard a badger snuffling and swaying its heavy weight further up.

Anna looked up at the trees, most of which were bare, and she saw the trees' arms and legs stretching and bending in many strange directions, silhouetted against the night-sky, which was now lighter than anything else they could see.

'Sshh', said Uncle Brad, and he pointed to two hedgehogs moving very swiftly along the gutter into the woodland, looking as if they knew exactly where they were going. They all watched until the hedgehogs sidled under the gate and made for their feeding ground. 'They'll be stocking up on food for their hibernation, foraging for snails, slugs, earthworms and beetles. You don't often see a hedgehog during the day.'

Timothy said he could hear the stream running underneath the road and was astonished to realise that he'd never heard it previously, despite having been to Bodnant many times before. But of course, never at night, in the dark, when your senses are very alert, and when you can hear and see things you might miss in the daylight.

Then to finish off the night-time show, the silver moon came out from behind a cloud and for just a moment, its light made everything look as if it were covered in salt.

Suddenly the sky became alive with hundreds and hundreds of tiny black creatures flying back and forth to their homes: old buildings, trees, and bat-boxes.

'Bats,' said Timothy's dad. 'What a sight!'

'I always wonder why they don't collide,' said Mrs Crumble.

'Well, they have a complicated sound system which signals to each of them so that they don't fly into each other.'

'I can't hear them signaling to each other,' Timothy said. 'Not even when I'm listening really hard.

'Ah, you won't, even when you're really, really listening hard. The bats' ultrasonic sounds are not audible to the human ear. So, all that traffic-control in the sky is managed by sounds which humans can't hear.'

'We've seen and heard such a lot this evening,' said Timothy's mum. 'I'm really pleased you suggested it,' she told Timothy's dad. 'We must do it again sometime.'

'Let's have one more look around,' said Aunt Prim. 'And then, it's home for us all.'

Timothy, William, George, Anna and Ishbel looked up and around, trying to see if they'd missed anything. Their eyes were as bright in the moonlight as Benji's had been when they arrived.

'Did you enjoy your night-time adventure?' Timothy asked his brother. But now, Benji's eyes were closed. He was fast asleep.

YOUR ACTIVITY PAGE

TIMOTHY CRUMBLE AND THE EXPLORERS

This last story is in the form of a poem and written in a style which you might recognise as being like the *Rupert Bear* stories. Rupert Bear has been around for a very long time and has been illustrated by many artists – one of them was Mr. Alfred Bestall, who drew Rupert and his human and animal friends in a land not dis-similar to Bodnant Garden.

Much of the landscape he drew so beautifully was inspired by the Snowdonia landscape – this is not surprising because

Alfred Bestall lived in the Conwy Valley in Trefriw, and in Beddgelert!

The Rupert Bear stories are set in a village called Nutwood, and many of Rupert's adventures took place in a wild forest or large garden full of trees, flowers, and shrubs; secret paths, trails and caves leading to mysterious places. Alfred Bestall visited Bodnant Garden when he lived in Trefriw, and it's possible that when he drew Rupert and all his adventuring friends in the huge forest-like garden, he had Bodnant Garden in mind!

Rupert and his parents are what are known as, 'anthropomorphic' – that means they are animals with a humanoid form, his anthropomorphic friends include a badger, an elephant, and a mouse. He had some human friends too, and Raggety, a woodland troll-like-creature made from twigs!

Now, where have we heard about trolls before?

Hmm, yes, I remember! Timothy Crumble and his cousins, William and George Harker, looked for trolls in Bodnant Garden and didn't see **one**, but his two girl cousins, Anna and Ishbel, **did**!

So, Timothy Crumble and the explorers
To Bodnant did visit a lot
The month they arrived determined the prize
Of what they would see – or would not!

It might be the arch of sunshine-like flowers
It might be the bluebells – so blue
It might be the daffodils, yellow and cream
A golden host waving to you!

They'd race through the tunnel so safe now to cross
From car park to the entrance gate
Past the café and promises 'pon their return
For tea, scones, or scrumptious cake!

At the desk they found plans and maps all around
Of which way to go and see all
To the ha-ha, the Redwoods, the massive oak tree
To the river and great waterfall!

They went looking for trolls and a fairy or two
They found plants that were smelly and stank!
They saw graves that were special and kept for the
cats,
Under an old English Yew, dark and dank

Once, Timothy Crumble and his fine pals
Thought the Arch and Laburnum had gone!
All it was showing instead of the flowers
Were fingers and toes of sticks – brown

But later of course when the weeks had gone by
The yellow festoons hung well low

Timothy Crumble Explores Bodnant Garden

To dapple the ground and filter the sun
And put on its world-famous show

Timothy Crumble and his explorer friends
His cousins, called William and George
Their sisters, the girl twins, Anna and Ishbel –
A friendship was well truly forged

As children they come to see everything here
And learn, just as if in their schools
Of flowers and birds and bugs and strange scents
And at night-time, of ghosts, and of owls!

Of snail-trails and hunts, and creepy old haunts
Have you visited the Poem yet?
It's a funny old name for a mystery place
That holds memories of people long dead!

I hope, and I hope that you also do too
Appreciate Bodnant – it's rare!
To find such a garden in which to explore
A garden for which **you** can take care!

YOUR ACTIVITY PAGE

THE END

Author Biography

Anne Forrest lives in the Conwy Valley, North Wales. She gained a Masters at the University of Chester: 'Writing and Publishing Fiction' 2019-2020, after gaining a First Class Hons at Bangor Uni: MArts in 'English Literature with Creative Writing' in 2019. Her common-folk biography, *My Whole World, Penmaenmawr* was published by Old Bakehouse Publications, Abertillery, in 2000. *Lilies of the Valley*, a Gothic, family saga, made the strong longlist in the Cinnamon Press Debut Novel Award 2018, and her picaresque novel, *Quinn*, made the 'Mention with Honours' in 2020.

In partnership with co-writer, Judy Price, her collection of 'uncanny', short stories, *Cautiously Tiptoeing…Out of the Light*, was published in October 2020, and *Cautiously Tiptoeing…Into the Thirteen Days of Christmas*, in December.

Timothy Crumble Explores Bodnant Garden is her first children's book. Visit her website at;
http://anneforrestwriter.weebly.com.
Facebook pages: *Anne Forrest Writer* and, *Forrest & Price*

Illustrator Biography

Having studied fashion illustration & design at Manchester Metropolitan University, Laura Stenhouse is a free-lance illustrator and artist. She was selected for the Big Art Show for BBC and was runner up in the 'Young Designer of the Year' at the Clothes Show in 2001.

Formally a children's librarian, Laura has also worked on community art projects, and as a Creative Practitioner for the Welsh Arts Council.

Now working from home in North Wales, her work is available locally and can be seen at *Parliament of Owls* at https://www.facebook.com/OwlsofAthena. stenhouselaura@hotmail.co.uk

Thanks

My initial thanks must go to Bodnant Garden for the opportunity to write about Timothy Crumble as he explores their wonderful garden; the tales were used at a story-telling-time activity. My liaison with The National Trust has been one of help and co-operation.

Adults and children have critiqued the stories and I'm grateful for their input. I'm also indebted to others who've been generous with their support, their time and experience: Martin James, Stuart Kelly, and especially L. Lindee, and Judy Price (and everyone who led me to these people).

The children reading, or being read to, will bring the stories to life in their own imagination.

I'm very thrilled that the talented Laura Stenhouse worked with me to transfer my fictitious characters into magical reality.

Thank you.

Other publications by this author:

Collection of short-stories, co-written with Judy Price, **'Cautiously Tiptoeing...Out of the Light'** (Forrest & Price September 2020) and **'Cautiously Tiptoeing...Into the Thirteen Days of Christmas'** (Amazon KDP, Forrest & Price, December 2020)

'Transforming Communities: Waterloo Writing Festival,' eds. Debz Hobbs-Wyatt and Gill James (Bridgehouse Publications, 2020)

Anthology **'Not For Bedtime: Chilling Tales from around the world',** ed. Neil Gee, (Chester: Infinity Junction, 2001)

Common-folk Biography **'My Whole World, Penmaenmawr,'** (Abertillery: Old Bakehouse Publications, November 2000)

Printed in Great Britain
by Amazon